For Lizzie, of course
D.M.

For David, Penny,
and Lizzie
D.G.

Text © 1993 by David Martin
Illustrations © 1993 by Debi Gliori

First edition 1993

Library of Congress Cataloging-in-Publication Data

Martin, David, 1944-
Lizzie and her puppy / David Martin; illustrated by Debi Gliori. —1st ed.
Summary: Lizzie and her puppy have fun playing together in a box.
ISBN 1-56402-059-2
[1. Dogs—Fiction. 2. Play—Fiction. 3. Stories in rhyme.]
I. Gliori, Debi, ill. II. Title
PZ8.3.M4115Liz 1993 92-53008
[E]—dc20

10 9 8 7 6 5 4 3 2 1

Printed in Hong Kong

The pictures for this book were done in watercolor.

Candlewick Press
2067 Massachusetts Avenue
Cambridge, Massachusetts 02140

Lizzie
and Her Puppy

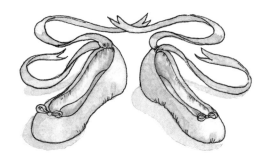

DAVID MARTIN

illustrated by
DEBI GLIORI

CANDLEWICK PRESS
CAMBRIDGE, MASSACHUSETTS

Where is Lizzie?
Lizzie's in the box.

What is Lizzie doing?
Taking off her socks.

Where is Lizzie's puppy?
Puppy's in the dirt.

What is puppy doing?
Chewing Lizzie's shirt.